NICK JR.
DORA the EXPLORER®

Dora and the Rainbow Kite Festival

by Christine Ricci   illustrated by Robert Roper

Ready-to-Read

SCHOLASTIC INC.

New York Toronto London Auckland Sydney
Mexico City New Delhi Hong Kong Buenos Aires

Based on the TV series *Dora the Explorer*® as seen on Nick Jr.®

ISBN-13: 978-0-545-04175-1
ISBN-10: 0-545-04175-9

12 11 10 9 8 7 6 5 4 3 2 1   8 9 10 11 12 13/0

Printed in the U.S.A.

First Scholastic printing, April 2008

Hi! I am .
DORA

Look! There is a .
KITE

stuck in that .
TREE

We have to help her!

How can we reach
the top of the 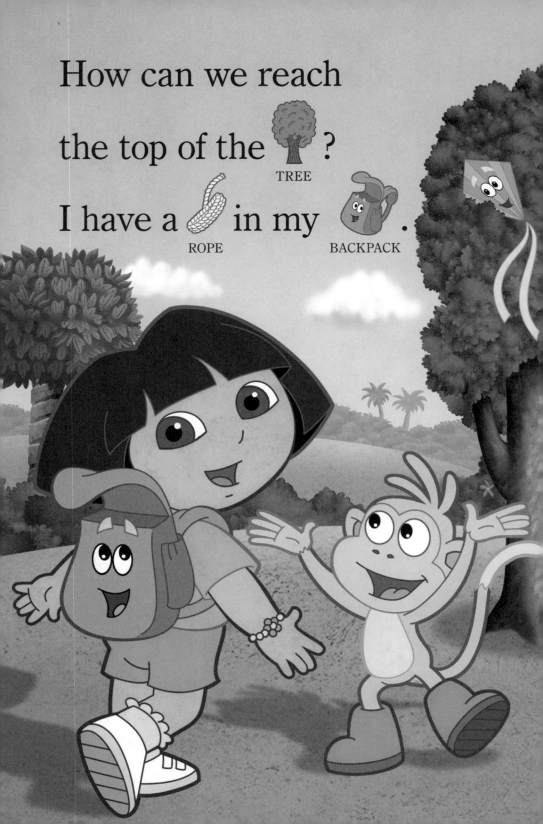?
TREE
I have a in my .
ROPE   BACKPACK

We need the longest .

ROPE

Do you see it?

is a great climber!

BOOTS

rescued the ▱ !

BOOTS   KITE

The  has to get to
KITE

the 🌈 🪁 Festival
RAINBOW KITE

before the 🌈 disappears.
RAINBOW

Will you help us?

How do we get to

the  RAINBOW KITE Festival?

Let's ask MAP!

 says the   Festival is
MAP   RAINBOW KITE

at the top of Tallest .
MOUNTAIN

First we go past the .
WINDMILL

Then we go through .
RAINBOW   DOOR

We made it to the  WINDMILL .

It is so windy!

We need to turn off the  WINDMILL

so the  KITE can fly by.

But the  WIND is blowing us

away from the  SWITCH.

I know!

I need to make a 🪢.
STRING   LASSO

Do you see any 🧵?
STRING

The little 🪁 has 🧵!
KITE   STRING

We lassoed the

SWITCH

and stopped the !

WIND

RAINBOW DOOR has **7** SEVEN LOCKS!

Can you find **7** SEVEN KEYS

to match the **7** SEVEN LOCKS?

Oh, no! I see .
SWIPER

He will try to swipe the .
KEYS

We have to stop him.

Say " , no swiping!"
SWIPER

We stopped ![SWIPER] !
SWIPER

The **7** ![SEVEN KEYS] opened
SEVEN KEYS

the **7** ![SEVEN LOCKS] on ![RAINBOW] ![DOOR] .
SEVEN LOCKS   RAINBOW   DOOR

Next comes Tallest MOUNTAIN.

There it is!

We have to hurry!

The RAINBOW is starting to fade!

Tallest  MOUNTAIN is so tall!

How can we get to the top?

The can fly us
KITE

to the top of the ⛰.
MOUNTAIN

We can hold on to her !
RIBBONS

We made it to the

 Festival!

RAINBOW KITE

All of the are so happy.

KITES

But where is the  ?

RAINBOW

Say "Come back,  !"

RAINBOW

The 🌈 heard us

RAINBOW

and came back.

Look at his colors!

The  are ready to fly.
KITES

Here they go!

Look at all of the  **KITES**

flying under the  **RAINBOW**!

We did it!

Thanks for helping!